Thad, the Talking Crayon

Table of Contents

1. **Title of Book** — Page 1
2. **Table of Contents** — Page 2
3. **Dedication's Page** — Page 3
4. **Story, Thad, the Talking Crayon** — Pages 4-36
5. **Brief book synopsis & Author bio** — Pages 37-38

Dedication's Page

This book is dedicated to my friends and family who have loved me more than I actually love myself.

This book is also dedicated to my betrothed, if and when I ever find him.

This book is also dedicated to all of the little children that have an active imagination such as myself.

It was a cold winter's day as Sydney, the talking train, pulled into the Crayon kingdom.
The wind was howling as it travelled throughout the little train station.
Sydney's wheels were tired and very old.
His paint was chipped in several places but his laughter could be heard for miles throughout the kingdom.

The train master just looked at Sydney and he smiled at him.

"Hello Sydney" the train master said.
"Hello Mr. Brooklyn" the little talking train replied.
"How are you doing today?"
Mr. Brooklyn told Sydney that he had been very busy for the last couple of days.
"It looks like it" Sydney said as he let out a loud chuckle.

"Woo, woo" he said again.
The entire Crayon kingdom knew that their safe passage had arrived.

Unknown to everyone, the Crayon kingdom was a very special town.
Their crayons were different from all of the others.
The crayons were gifted beyond measure.
They were actually capable of spreading happiness and cheer all over the world to very special children.
The Crayon kingdom would always allow one special crayon to accompany each box for a child.

Sydney rested his engine and tired, little wheels while the Crayon kingdom prepared their special boxes of crayons to distribute all over the world.

The little Crayon kingdom was in an exceptionally good mood that day.
They started production very early and everyone was being very productive indeed.
Everyone was whistling while they worked throughout the kingdom.

**The Crayon kingdom's foreman started early that morning.
He knew that it was going to be a special day since Sydney was arriving to take the kingdom's crayons all over the world.**

Nicholas opened the doors to the crayon plant and he heard the most magnificent singing coming from the design department.

**He smiled as he opened the door.
Nicholas saw all of the little crayons dancing around the designer's desk.
He just knew that this was going to be an exciting day.**

Nicholas watched as Sabrina held up the designs to get their opinions about what their boxes should look like.
She held up one box that was a bright yellow and the little crayon named Madison yelled from the crowd.
"I will take that box" she said.
"I simply love that color" she replied again.
"Can we add some pretty flowers to the box to spruce it up some?"

"Sure we can" Sabrina said smiling.

Sabrina held up the next design for a crayon box.
This time it was blue.
Othello yelled from the crayon crowd.

"I want that box" he said.
"Blue has always been my favorite color" Othello said again.
"Can I have some little trucks, baseballs and small fish on the crayon box?"
Sabrina just laughed at him.
"I would be happy to do that for you" she said to Othello.

"Wow, you guys are easy to please today" Sabrina said.
The crayons laughed with excitement then.
"Yeah, we know we're awesome" they all said in uniform voice.
Sabrina laughed at all of them then.
"You know it" Sabrina said again.
"You guys rock" she said again.
The crayons just laughed and began to dance around in their little chairs a little.

Sabrina held up the next box.
This box was very unique.
It had some red, green, and purple shades of color.

The crowd was silent just for a brief moment.
This was very rare in the Crayon kingdom.

At first, Sabrina didn't think that the little crayons liked that box. She was getting ready to discard it when a little voice told her to stop.

"I will take that box" Thad said.
"I think that crayon box is a magnificent creation" he said again.
Sabrina thanked him politely.

Everyone in the little crayon crowd listened as Thad began to speak.

He told Sabrina that he liked unique boxes to draw more attention.

The crayons agreed with him.

"I never looked at it like that" one crayon replied.

"Me either" another said.

Thad and Sabrina just laughed at all of them.

"What would you like on your box Thad?"
"I would like some kaleidoscopes on my box" Thad said.

"Alright Thad" Sabrina replied.

Thad thanked Sabrina politely and then he began to move in a zig zag pattern on her desk.

"I can't wait to see what special child gets me" Thad said. Everyone just laughed at him them.

The workday ended right after that.
Sabrina worked most of the evening preparing the special box requests from the little Crayon kingdom.
She absolutely loved her job.
The little crayons were so happy and they always made her day.

Early the next morning, the crayons gathered in the loading dock.

**They were eager to evaluate Sabrina's final box creations.
Madison squealed with crayon delight as she gazed at the beautiful flowers Sabrina had added.
She began to squiggle dance on the table.
She loved her new box.**

Othello waited patiently as Sabrina pulled out his box.
"Wow, that is so cool" Othello said.
He glanced at the designs that had been created for him.
He began to do a belly roll on the table.

Everyone laughed again.
"Yippee" he said.

Sabrina pulled out the unique box that Thad had chosen one day earlier.

All of the crayons gasped as they visualized Thad's box.

Thad was nowhere to be found at first.

All of a sudden, everyone looked to their left.

Thad was skating down the loading dock, grinning from ear to ear.

"Now that is what I am talking about" Thad replied.

"That crayon box speaks to me" he said.

"I can't wait to see what my special child thinks about my box" he said.

Everyone just laughed at him.

He immediately jumped into his box as he hummed a little tune.

All of the little crayons in the Crayon kingdom loved all of Sabrina's creative crayon designs.

Sabrina thanked all of them.
She was so happy so could assist them with their new crayon boxes.
All of the other crayons jumped right into their boxes as they began to be loaded onto Sydney, the talking train.

Sydney let out a loud laugh as his engine whistle blew.
His laughter echoed throughout the entire Crayon kingdom then.
His steam oiled his wheels once more.
Sydney smiled at all of the little crayons.
He was so proud that he could carry them to their destination.

All of the crayons knew it was time to meet their special child.
The little crayons were excited about their new project.
Sydney dropped Madison off in New York.
He dropped Othello off in Ohio.
Thad was dropped off in New Jersey.

Thad was excited as he was placed on the shelves at a large retail store.

His little box really stood out on the shelf.

He was very proud of himself and his designs that Sabrina had made for him.

After a couple of days, a little girl looked up from a shopping cart and squealed with happiness.

"Mommy, can I have some new crayons?"

"Of course dear" her mother replied.
"My, that box is bright and colorful" she said again.
The little girl smiled at her mother then.
"I love that crayon box" the little girl said.
"I see why" her mother replied again.

When they got home, the little girl immediately took her new crayons to her room.

Her mom made her a snack for lunch and she went right to her room.

She was eager to check out her new box of crayons.

She didn't know that her new crayon box had a small surprise waiting for her.

The little girl touched the crayon box softly and she began to inspect all of the kaleidoscope designs.

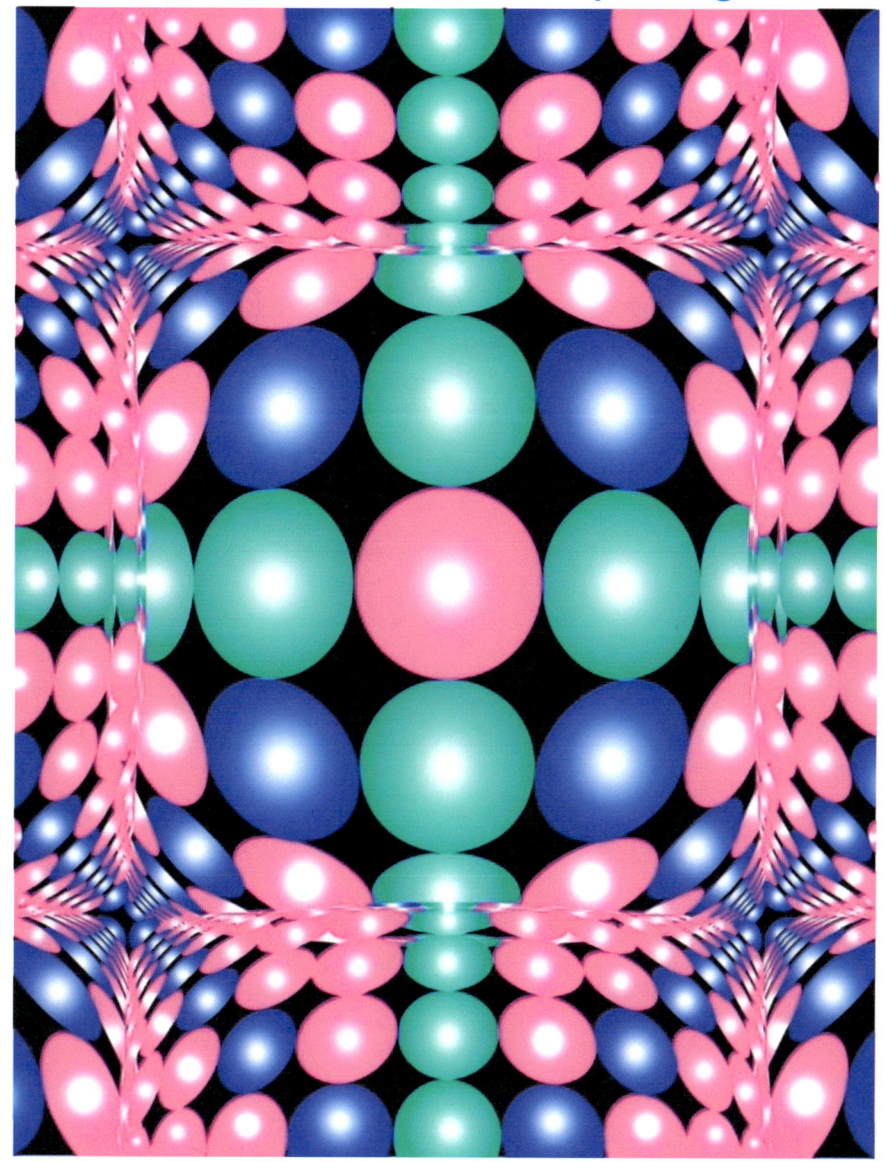

"Wow, this crayon box is so awesome" she said.
"I just knew you would like my box" Thad said.
The box began to bounce around a little and the little girl was taken aback but only briefly.
"Huh?" "Are you talking to me?"
The little girl began to scratch her head a little.

"Go ahead and open the box" Thad said.
The little girl looked shocked.
Thad just laughed then.
The little girl smiled as a small child would.
She decided she was going to take the crayon boxes advice and she opened her new box of crayons.

Thad immediately jumped right out of the box and began his introduction dance.

He danced around and performed a squiggle dance for her.
The little girl giggled happily.
"Shoo" he said.
"I was getting a little cramped in my box" he said.
The little girl giggled again.

"What's your name?"
"My name is Paige" the little girl replied.
"Hi Paige" Thad said.
"My name is Thad" the little crayon said.
Thad asked Paige if she wanted to be friends.
The little girl nodded her head eagerly.
"Yes" she said without hesitation.

"Wow, you have a nice room" Thad said.
"Thank you Thad" she said to the little crayon.
They both giggled then.

"How do you know how to talk?"
Thad shrugged his little crayon shoulders then.
"I don't know" he said.
Paige just laughed at him again.

Paige began to rub her eyes. She thought that she may be imaging this conversation with the little crayon.

**She was glad to have Thad as a friend though.
She got so lonely playing by herself.
"I really liked your box Thad" Paige said to him again.
"Why thank you Paige" he said.
"Now it's your crayon box too" he said again.**

Thad knew that he had found his special child.
He was so happy.
This was his crayon destiny.
Every day Paige would draw a picture and they would color together.

Sometimes Thad would jump out of the crayon box and zig zag on some paper and Paige would just squeal with child delight.

This made Thad very happy and Paige was so happy that she had found her little talking crayon.

Sometimes, he would glide down the chair to cheer her up.
"Wee" he said.
Paige would clap her hands with happiness.
Sometimes he would roll around on her desk to get her attention and it worked every time.

Paige would just smile and they would play for a while.
They would also sing together.
Paige would draw houses aligned with flowers or other precious things in the eyes of a child.

Thad would help her color each and every time.
They both knew that they would be best friends for life!

The End

The Crayon kingdom was a very special town. Each year they would send out one special crayon in search of a very special child. Paige got lonely playing by herself all of the time. One day she asked her mother if she could have a new box of crayons. Unknown to Paige, the special crayon box she chose had a little surprise for her!

Misty Lynn Wesley was born in Chicago and raised in West Virginia. She has several diplomas, certificates, and degrees in the medical and legal industries as well as other fields of interest. Her love for children and the active imagination of childhood innocence were her inspirations in writing this Children's book. Please be sure to check out all of her other Children's books, Christian books and crime novels as well. You will be glad that you did! God bless all of you.

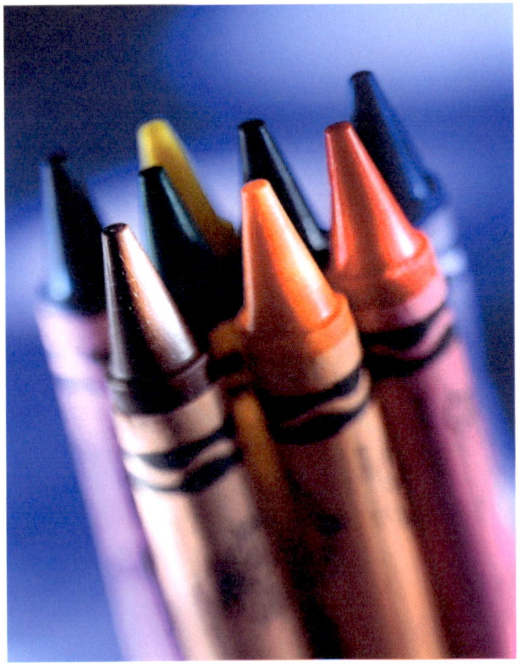

Made in the USA
Columbia, SC
23 February 2025